The Boxcar Children Mysteries

THE BOXCAR CHILDREN
SURPRISE ISLAND
THE YELLOW HOUSE MYSTERY
MYSTERY RANCH
MIKE'S MYSTERY
BLUE BAY MYSTERY
THE WOODSHED MYSTERY
THE LIGHTHOUSE MYSTERY
MOUNTAIN TOP MYSTERY
SCHOOLHOUSE MYSTERY
CABOOSE MYSTERY
HOUSEBOAT MYSTERY
SNOWBOUND MYSTERY
TREE HOUSE MYSTERY
BICYCLE MYSTERY
MYSTERY IN THE SAND
MYSTERY BEHIND THE WALL
BUS STATION MYSTERY
BENNY UNCOVERS A MYSTERY
THE HAUNTED CABIN
   MYSTERY
THE DESERTED LIBRARY
   MYSTERY
THE ANIMAL SHELTER
   MYSTERY
THE OLD MOTEL MYSTERY
THE MYSTERY OF THE HIDDEN
   PAINTING
THE AMUSEMENT PARK
   MYSTERY
THE MYSTERY OF THE MIXED-
   UP ZOO

THE CAMP-OUT MYSTERY
THE MYSTERY GIRL
THE MYSTERY CRUISE
THE DISAPPEARING FRIEND
   MYSTERY
THE MYSTERY OF THE SINGING
   GHOST
MYSTERY IN THE SNOW
THE PIZZA MYSTERY
THE MYSTERY HORSE
THE MYSTERY AT THE DOG
   SHOW
THE CASTLE MYSTERY
THE MYSTERY OF THE LOST
   VILLAGE
THE MYSTERY ON THE ICE
THE MYSTERY OF THE
   PURPLE POOL
THE GHOST SHIP MYSTERY
THE MYSTERY IN
   WASHINGTON, DC
THE CANOE TRIP MYSTERY
THE MYSTERY OF THE HIDDEN
   BEACH
THE MYSTERY OF THE MISSING
   CAT
THE MYSTERY AT SNOWFLAKE
   INN
THE MYSTERY ON STAGE
THE DINOSAUR MYSTERY
THE MYSTERY OF THE STOLEN
   MUSIC

THE MYSTERY AT THE BALL PARK

THE CHOCOLATE SUNDAE MYSTERY

THE MYSTERY OF THE HOT AIR BALLOON

THE MYSTERY BOOKSTORE

THE PILGRIM VILLAGE MYSTERY

THE MYSTERY OF THE STOLEN BOXCAR

MYSTERY IN THE CAVE

THE MYSTERY ON THE TRAIN

THE MYSTERY AT THE FAIR

THE MYSTERY OF THE LOST MINE

THE GUIDE DOG MYSTERY

THE HURRICANE MYSTERY

THE PET SHOP MYSTERY

THE MYSTERY OF THE SECRET MESSAGE

THE FIREHOUSE MYSTERY

THE MYSTERY IN SAN FRANCISCO

THE NIAGARA FALLS MYSTERY

THE MYSTERY AT THE ALAMO

THE OUTER SPACE MYSTERY

THE SOCCER MYSTERY

THE MYSTERY IN THE OLD ATTIC

THE GROWLING BEAR MYSTERY

THE MYSTERY OF THE LAKE MONSTER

THE MYSTERY AT PEACOCK HALL

THE WINDY CITY MYSTERY

THE BLACK PEARL MYSTERY

THE CEREAL BOX MYSTERY

THE PANTHER MYSTERY

THE MYSTERY OF THE QUEEN'S JEWELS

THE STOLEN SWORD MYSTERY

THE BASKETBALL MYSTERY

THE MOVIE STAR MYSTERY

THE MYSTERY OF THE PIRATE'S MAP

THE GHOST TOWN MYSTERY

THE MYSTERY OF THE BLACK RAVEN

THE MYSTERY IN THE MALL

THE MYSTERY IN NEW YORK

THE GYMNASTICS MYSTERY

THE POISON FROG MYSTERY

THE MYSTERY OF THE EMPTY SAFE

THE HOME RUN MYSTERY

THE GREAT BICYCLE RACE MYSTERY

THE MYSTERY OF THE WILD PONIES

THE MYSTERY IN THE COMPUTER GAME

THE MYSTERY AT THE CROOKED HOUSE

THE HOCKEY MYSTERY

THE MYSTERY OF THE MIDNIGHT DOG

THE MYSTERY OF THE SCREECH OWL

THE SUMMER CAMP MYSTERY

THE COPYCAT MYSTERY

THE HAUNTED CLOCK TOWER MYSTERY

THE HAUNTED CLOCK TOWER MYSTERY

created by

GERTRUDE CHANDLER WARNER

Illustrated by Hodges Soileau

SCHOLASTIC INC.
New York Toronto London Auckland Sydney
New Delhi Mexico City Hong Kong Buenos Aires

ISBN 0-439-24096-4

12 11 10 9 8 7 6 5 4 3 2   1 2 3 4 5 6/0

Printed in the U.S.A.   40
First Scholastic printing, September 2001

Contents

CHAPTER   PAGE

1. The Tower   1
2. A Strange Light at Midnight   17
3. A Ghost in the Tower   31
4. Do Ghosts Wear Sneakers?   47
5. Buried Treasure!   58
6. Going on a Treasure Hunt   74
7. Guess Who's Coming to Dinner!   91
8. The Tower Points the Way   108
9. The Professor's Secret Project   120
10. A Reward for the Children   130

CHAPTER 1

The Tower

"I think I see it!" shouted Benny Alden, pointing out the car window.

"I do, too!" called his sister Violet, who was sitting beside him.

"Yes, that's it!" said their grandfather, James Alden. He steered the car up a hill. "That's the famous clock tower."

Benny was only six years old and Violet was ten, but they were on their way to college. Their grandfather was taking them to visit Goldwin University, where he had studied forty years before. He was back for his weeklong class reunion and had brought his four grandchildren with him. Twelve-year-old Jessie and fourteen-year-old Henry looked out the car window, too. A tall clock tower loomed over their car and over the whole campus of Goldwin University.

James Alden was the children's grandfather, but he had been more like a father to them ever since their parents had died. At first the children had been afraid to go live with him, because they thought he would be mean. So they ran away and lived in an old boxcar in the woods. But when they discovered what a kind man their grandfather was, they came to live with him in his big house in Greenfield. And he even brought the boxcar and put it in their backyard, so they could use it as a playhouse.

The family had been driving for nearly five hours. Everyone was happy when they finally arrived.

"It's even more beautiful here than in the pictures you showed us," said Jessie, looking at the beautiful stone buildings covered with ivy.

Grandfather pulled into a parking lot. Directly in front of them was the tall, narrow clock tower, ten stories high.

"Can we go up there?" asked Henry.

"Sure," said Grandfather as they all got out. "It will feel good to stretch our legs. From the top you can see the whole campus. I can point out the building where I had my classes, the dining hall where I ate my meals, and the dormitory where I lived. That's where we'll be staying this week."

"How do we get up there?" Benny wanted to know.

"We take the stairs," said Grandfather.

"Stairs?" repeated Benny, craning his neck to look at the top of the tower again. "There's no elevator?"

"No, just stairs," said Grandfather, grinning. "Lots of them."

"One hundred sixty-one, to be exact," said a voice behind them.

The Aldens turned to see a man standing there. He was about Grandfather's age, with thick white hair and a long white beard. He was neatly dressed in a dark suit with a red-

and-white vest and matching bow tie. The school colors were red and white, and Jessie noticed his tie was decorated with tiny bears, the Goldwin mascot. The man wore shiny tasseled loafers.

"I'm Ezra Stewart," the man said, putting out his hand for Grandfather to shake. "You must be an old Goldwin student, back for the reunion."

"Yes, I am. And these are my grandchildren." Grandfather introduced each of them.

"Mr. Stewart, how did you know how many stairs there are inside the clock tower?" asked Jessie.

"Because I go up and down those stairs at least twice a day," Ezra said. "I'm the carillon player."

"The what?" Benny asked.

Ezra smiled. "I play the carillon — the bells in the tower. My assistant and I give three concerts a day: morning, noon, and evening. I take care of the bells and the clock as well."

"I used to love to wake up to the carillon

music when I was a student here," Grandfather recalled.

"Come on up, I'll show you," Ezra said. "But you have to promise me one thing."

"All right," Henry agreed. "What is it?"

"You must call me Ezra," he said.

"Okay, Ezra," said Benny. "But do we really have to walk up one hundred and — how many stairs was it?"

"One hundred sixty-one," said Ezra. "And you don't have to walk. You can run. I'll race you!" he called over his shoulder as he set off toward a door in the bottom of the tower.

Benny grinned as he took off after Ezra.

The door was made of thick, solid wood. The tower looked as if it had been built long ago. Inside was a narrow, winding stairway. The stairs went around and around in a tight spiral. It was dark because there were only a few lights, and only a few narrow windows cut into the thick stone walls. The rest of the Aldens followed Benny and Ezra at a slower pace. Around and around, up and up they walked. Their footsteps echoed on the stone steps. It was difficult to move quickly in such a tight spiral on the small, uneven stairs.

"This is kind of creepy," Violet said.

"Don't worry," Jessie said. "I'm sure we'll get to the top soon."

A few minutes later, they were standing at the top of the tower in a small room with tiny windows on all four sides. They were a little bit dizzy and slightly out of breath from the climb. Violet was happy to be out of the stairway, although this dusty little room wasn't much better.

Henry went to one of the windows and looked out. "Wow!" he said. "What a view!"

"It is quite spectacular, isn't it?" Grandfather agreed. "I think it's the most beautiful college campus in the country."

"Of course it is," Ezra agreed wholeheartedly.

"What's that big green lawn down there?" Benny asked, looking out another window.

The children all crowded around the window and looked where Benny was pointing. There was a green lawn crisscrossed by sidewalks.

"That's the Quad," said Grandfather. "*Quad* is short for 'quadrangle,' which means a four-sided shape."

Benny quickly counted. "Yes, it does have four sides."

"What's that big building down there with the dome?" Violet wanted to know.

"That's where the largest classes are held," said Ezra.

"And what are those smaller buildings on either side of it?" Henry asked.

"Those are Morrill and McGraw Halls, where I had several of my classes," Grandfather said. "The one on the northern side of the Quad is Morrill; the one on the southern side is McGraw. And it looks like they're building a new building on the other end." He pointed to a building that was still under construction.

"Where was your room, Grandfather?" Violet wanted to know.

"Do you see that big hill?" he replied. "We called that the Slope. The dormitories are down there, and so is the dining hall."

At last the children turned away from the window to look at the room they were standing in. The walls were filled with framed pictures of the university. Many of the photographs were quite old and had a brownish tint.

Just then the clock chimed loudly.

"It's almost time for the evening concert," said Ezra. "Would you kids like to watch me play the carillon?"

"You bet!" cried Benny. "Is that it?" He pointed to the large wooden console in the center of the room.

"Yes, that's the carillon," Ezra said. "The bells are upstairs. We'll go up in a minute so you can see them. They're the best part — you won't believe how big they are."

The children had never seen anything quite like the carillon before. It reminded them a little bit of their upright piano at home. Just like their piano, it had a music stand on the front. Underneath the stand, instead of a keyboard, there were two long horizontal rows of wooden knobs sticking out. Down near the floor was a row of wooden pedals, and up above the carillon was a row of wires leading up through the ceiling.

"How does it work?" Jessie asked.

"You sit on this bench to play it," Ezra said as he sat down. "When you press down a knob or a pedal, a bell rings. Like this," he said, pressing down on the far-left knob. The children heard a bell chime above them.

"That's really neat," said Henry.

"Can I try?" Benny asked.

"Sure," Ezra said.

Benny carefully pressed down one of the knobs in the middle. Again the Aldens heard a bell ringing over their heads.

"Now let's go see the bells," Ezra suggested.

The Aldens followed Ezra out of the tower room. A small dark stairway took them to the floor above, where the bells were housed. There were two rows of large heavy bells on the bottom and two rows of smaller bells hanging above.

"That one on the end is bigger than me!" Benny cried.

"And it weighs a lot more, too," said Ezra. "It weighs more than forty-five hundred pounds! Would you like to go inside it?"

Benny's eyes grew wide. "Can I really?"

"Sure," Ezra said.

Benny bent down and ducked underneath the edge of the heavy bell. When he stood up inside, all the others could see were his legs sticking out at the bottom. "Hello out there!" he called. His voice had a strange muffled sound from inside the bell. Finally he ducked down and came back out. "I've never stood inside a bell before," he said.

"We have forty-nine bells here, which makes this carillon one of the largest in the country," Ezra said.

"So how does the carillon play these bells?" Violet wanted to know.

"Good question," Ezra said. "Did you notice those wires that came out of the carillon and through the ceiling? They come out here." He pointed to the row of wires

on the floor next to the bells. "Each wire is attached to a clapper inside a bell. When you press a knob on the carillon, the wire pulls the clapper on the bell." He pulled one of the wires with his fingers to show them. The clapper hit the side of the bell and made a ringing sound. "Each bell is specially made to play a different tone. When you play them together, you can make beautiful music."

"That's wonderful," Jessie said.

"In all the years I was here I heard a lot of concerts, but I never knew how it worked," Grandfather said. "Thank you for showing this to us."

"Would you like to go back downstairs now and watch me play the evening concert?" Ezra asked.

"We sure would," said Henry, speaking for the whole family.

Back downstairs, Violet asked Ezra, "How did you learn to play?"

"I learned a long time ago, when I was still a student here. I practiced on that console there." Ezra walked over to what looked like a smaller carillon in the corner. The children noticed that it had knobs just like the other one, but there were no wires attached. "This isn't attached to the bells, so you can practice without the whole school hearing you. It just rings on these metal plates above." Ezra pressed a knob, and they heard a clanging sound, like a xylophone. "This is where I've taught all my assistants.

"And now I'd better get out my music for the concert," Ezra said. He began sifting through some stacks of papers on a large desk next to the practice carillon. After a few minutes, he still had not found what he was looking for. He became angrier and angrier. "Where did Miss Barton put it?" he muttered to himself.

"Is something wrong?" Violet asked. Ezra had been so friendly and nice before, and now all of a sudden he seemed like a different person.

"It's this new assistant I have." He sighed. "She's a student named Andrea Barton. I like things to be a certain way up here. After all, I've been doing this for over fifty years — since I was a student myself. After a concert I always put the music back, in alphabetical order, on this desk. There isn't much space up here, so you have to be organized. But she always mixes everything up. Nothing has been the same up here since she started."

"Can I help you look?" Violet asked.

"No, no, no, I'll find it myself," said Ezra, sounding annoyed. "Oh, that girl makes me angry," he said under his breath.

"I'm sorry," said Violet in a quiet voice.

Ezra looked up, surprised. "Not you, dear," he said. "I was talking about Miss Barton." At last he pulled a stack of papers from the pile. "Ah, here it is."

He sat down on the carillon bench and the Aldens gathered around him. After placing the music on the stand, he opened to the first page. Then he began to play. The Aldens watched, fascinated. Ezra's hands, closed into fists, moved rapidly up and down the row of knobs. His hands crossed over and under each other as he pressed one knob after another with the sides of his fists. At the same time, his feet worked the pedals. From above, they could hear beautiful music.

After Ezra finished the first piece, Jessie said, "That looks like hard work."

"It is," Ezra said. "I've got calluses on the sides of my hands." He showed them how his hands had grown tough on the sides he used to press the knobs. "When I first started playing, I used to wrap my hands in bandages and wear gloves. But now I'm used to it."

Ezra went on to play several more pieces, each more beautiful and difficult than the one before. After half an hour, he played a piece the children recognized.

"That's the school anthem, isn't it?" Henry asked. "We've heard Grandfather singing it."

"Yes, it is," said Ezra.

As the hum from the last notes hung in the air above them, the Aldens applauded.

"Thank you," Ezra said, bowing his head slightly.

Just then there was a creaking noise from up above.

"What was that?" Benny asked, his eyes wide open. "I thought we were the only ones up here."

"This old tower creaks and groans all the time," said Ezra. "Some say it's haunted." His eyes twinkled, but his voice was serious.

"I remember those stories," Grandfather said. "The ghost in the clock tower."

"Aren't you scared to come up here by yourself?" Benny asked. "Like at night?"

Ezra looked sharply at Benny. "Well, I certainly don't come up here at night. No one does. Ever."

CHAPTER 2

A Strange Light at Midnight

After the Aldens left the tower, they picked up the key to their suite and drove to the dormitory.

"That tower was really neat," Henry said as they were driving.

"But a little spooky," Benny said.

"You don't believe there's really a ghost, do you?" Henry asked.

"Um, no," Benny said, but he didn't sound too sure.

"Ezra was just teasing," Jessie said. "He was nice."

"Yes, he was," Violet agreed. "Except when he was talking about his assistant, Andrea Barton. Then he seemed so different."

"That's true — he said that nothing has been the same there since she started working," Jessie remembered. "He said she messes everything up."

"He did seem like he was very neat and orderly about everything," Henry said. "You could tell by the way he was dressed."

When they arrived at the dormitory parking lot, Grandfather looked up at the red-brick building in front of them. "Good old Sage Hall," he said softly.

"It's about time you showed up!" said a man striding across the parking lot, his arms held out wide.

"Joel Dixon!" said Grandfather as he and the man embraced, patting each other firmly on the back.

"And these must be your grandchildren," said Joel, stepping back to look at them. "Don't tell me. This is Henry, and Jessie, and Violet."

Each child nodded and smiled as Grandfather's friend said his or her name.

"And this young fellow must be Benny," Joel said.

"You've got that right!" Benny said with a smile.

"This is my old college buddy Joel," Grandfather said.

Joel was a large man with dark hair, a friendly smile, and a big belly.

"We've heard a lot about you," Henry said.

"On the car ride up here our grandfather told us about all the crazy things you two used to do," said Benny, grinning.

"Your grandfather and I had a good time, didn't we, Jimbo?" said Joel. The children smiled. They weren't used to hearing their grandfather called by a nickname. "You didn't tell them about the time I lost the key to our room and had to climb in the window — did you?"

"He sure did," said Benny with a laugh.

"Oh, he did, did he?" asked Joel. "Well,

then, did he tell you about the time he took some frogs from the science lab and hid them in my bed?" Joel asked.

"You screamed so loud!" Grandfather said, laughing.

Everyone laughed, and Grandfather thumped Joel on the back affectionately.

"So, when did you get here?" Grandfather asked.

"Just a few minutes ago," Joel replied. "I was just coming back to check my car and make sure my son and I hadn't forgotten anything. Don's upstairs in our suite. He had some business in this area, so he's joining me for the reunion."

"That's great — I haven't seen Don in a long time," said Grandfather. "Let's go on up." He quickly got the suitcases out of the back of the car. "We're in Suite B-8," he said, leading the way.

"Great — Don and I are right next door, in B-10," Joel said.

The children followed their grandfather and Joel into Suite B-8.

"Oh, look — we can even cook here!"

Jessie said when she spotted the kitchen area at the end of the room. It had a small refrigerator and stove, and a small round table.

"Yes, that way we won't have to eat all our meals at the dining hall," said Grandfather.

Off the living room were three smaller rooms, each containing two twin beds.

"One room for the girls, one for the boys, and the third for Grandfather," said Jessie.

"That's right," said Grandfather as they each put their suitcases in their rooms.

"These rooms are nice," said Violet.

"This was where the upperclassmen — the older students — lived," Grandfather explained. "It looks like they've fixed them up a lot since I was here," he added with a chuckle, admiring the new windows and carpeting.

"Look!" Benny said, pointing out the window. "You can see the clock tower from here!" The Aldens looked up the hill and saw the tower at the top, outlined against the darkening sky.

"Come next door," Joel said. "We'll get

Don, and then we can all go to dinner together. They're having a special welcome
meal in the dining hall."

"Great!" said Benny. "I'm starving."

"You're always starving," said Jessie.

Everyone headed next door. Sitting on
the couch in Joel's suite was a large, dark-
haired man reading a book. The children
knew he had to be Joel's son because he
looked so much like him.

"Don!" Joel said. "The Aldens are here."

Don stood up quickly. He looked concerned, but his face quickly brightened
when he saw Grandfather. He closed his
book and tucked it quickly behind his back.
"James Alden, good to see you," he said. He
awkwardly transferred the book he'd been
holding to his left hand and put out his
right to shake Grandfather's.

"It's been too long," Grandfather said.

"I was just, uh . . . reading," Don said.
He looked slightly uncomfortable.

"Still reading that book I got you?" Joel
asked his son. He turned to the others. "It's
so funny. For years I've been trying to get

Don to come visit my old school, and he was never interested. But then I gave him this book, and suddenly he couldn't wait to come!"

Joel laughed his big, friendly laugh. He went to take the book from his son and show it to the Aldens, but Don didn't seem to want to let go of it. Instead Don held the book up for them to see. Printed on the faded leather cover were the words GOLD-WIN UNIVERSITY.

"That book looks really old," said Jessie. "Where did you find it?"

"In an antique store," Joel said. "It's over one hundred years old!"

"Wow!" said Benny. "Can I look at it?"

"I thought we were going to dinner," Don said quickly, putting the book out of reach on a high shelf.

Benny was sorry not to get a look at the book, but he was always ready to eat. "Dinner sounds great!"

Goldwin's main dining hall was right next to the clock tower. A large sign over the heavy wooden doors said, WELCOME ALUMNI!

Grandfather looked around as they walked inside. Then he smiled at Joel. "Hasn't changed a bit," he said.

"What are alum — alum — whatever that word is?" asked Benny.

"Alumni are people who graduated from this school," Grandfather explained. "Like Joel and me. Look, Joel — there's where we sign in."

They stopped at a table that was set up by the door and were given a schedule of the week's events and name tags for the whole family.

"Something smells good!" Joel said after he'd put on his name tag.

"Sure does," Benny agreed.

Joel led the way over to the counter and handed everyone a tray. One by one, they all walked down the buffet line, selecting what they wanted to eat. There was pot roast, chicken, potatoes and vegetables, fresh fruit, and Jell-O in all different colors.

When they'd filled their trays, Grandfather noticed an empty table near the windows. "Let's go sit over there."

They had just sat down when an elderly woman walked by holding a tray. As she passed their table, she stopped short and her eyes opened wide. "Well, if it isn't Jimmy Alden!" she said, smiling broadly. The woman was wearing a brightly colored dress, a floppy hat with a large pink flower on it, and bright pink sneakers to match.

Mr. Alden looked at her for a moment before realizing who it was. "Professor Meyer!" he said at last. "My favorite history teacher."

"I hoped my star pupil would remember me," she said, resting her tray on their table. "You know, you can call me Julia now that you're not in my class."

"And I hope you remember me, too," said Joel.

"Of course I do — Joel Dixon!" said Professor Meyer. "I rarely saw you and Jimmy apart. I'm so glad to see you're still good friends."

Jessie giggled. "It's funny to hear people call Grandfather 'Jimmy.' "

"So you're Jimmy's grandchildren, are you?" the professor asked her.

"Yes. I'm Jessie, and this is Henry, Benny, and Violet." Jessie motioned to each of her brothers and her sister in turn.

"It sure is nice to meet you," Professor Meyer said, adjusting her hat.

"Professor Meyer knows everything about this college," Grandfather told the children.

"Everything?" Don asked, leaning forward in his chair.

"I probably do," Julia agreed. "After all, I've been here a long time — over fifty years! I always thought I'd leave one day, maybe get a job where I could make a little more money. But that's okay. Now I'm working on — oh, let's just call it my special project — maybe I'll be able to make a little money without ever leaving Goldwin." She smiled and raised her eyebrows as she picked up her tray. "I'm sure I'll see you again this week!"

"It was nice meeting you," Violet said as the professor walked away.

"I wonder what her special project is," said Henry.

"It certainly did sound a little mysterious," Joel said.

"Don't start talking about mysteries with these kids," warned Grandfather. "They are master mystery solvers!"

"Really?" said Don. "I'm a mystery solver, too."

"Yes, Don was always playing detective as a kid," Joel agreed.

"Tell us about yours," Don said to the kids.

As they ate, the Aldens told Joel and Don about some of the exciting adventures they'd had, like the time they traveled to England and found the queen's jewels, and the time Jessie joined a hockey team coached by a hockey superstar. Don told them about the mysteries he'd solved when he was young. After they'd all finished eating, they still sat and talked for a long time. Grandfather and Joel Dixon recognized many people walking by who had been their friends years before.

"Grandfather sure did have a lot of friends in college," Benny said.

It was dark when the Aldens and the Dixons finally left the dining hall. As they came out of the building, they saw the clock tower directly in front of them, lit up against the night sky. A golden full moon shone high above the tower.

"Wow, look at that!" said Jessie, her eyes wide. "It looks even cooler at night than during the day."

"It sure does," Henry agreed.

"I wouldn't be surprised if it really was haunted," said Benny. He stared up at the windows of the clock tower. The room at the top looked dark and empty.

"Haunted!" Joel said. "That boy sure has a good imagination, Jim."

"Yes, he does," Grandfather agreed, tousling Benny's hair.

Benny laughed with the others. But as they walked back down the hill, he couldn't

help taking one last peek over his shoulder at the moonlit tower.

When the Aldens got back to their suite, they were worn out from their long day. In no time they were all asleep.

In the middle of the night, Benny woke up feeling thirsty. He rubbed his eyes and looked at the clock beside his bed. It was midnight. Benny slowly walked to the bathroom and got himself a drink of water.

As he was heading back to bed, Benny walked past the window. He stopped to look at the clock tower standing at the top of the hill. The full moon was now directly behind it. The clock face was shining brightly, as before, but something had changed. A dim light was glowing in the window at the top of the tower. Benny could see a shadowy figure moving around.

"Oh, my goodness!" Benny said softly to himself. "There's someone up there! But Ezra said no one's up there at night."

Suddenly Benny had another thought. "What if it's the ghost?"

CHAPTER 3

A Ghost in the Tower

Benny rushed over to Henry's bed. "Henry! Henry! Wake up!"

"Who — what — ?" Henry said, startled, sitting up quickly in bed, clutching his blankets. "Benny, what's going on?"

"Henry, there's somebody up in the tower! I think it's a ghost!" Benny explained.

"What are you talking about?" Henry asked.

"Come here! Look!" Benny cried, taking Henry by the hand and pulling him over to the window. "See?" He pointed up at the clock tower.

Henry rubbed his sleepy eyes and looked where Benny was pointing. "Yes? So?" he said sleepily.

"Don't you see?" Benny asked. "There's a light on, and it's midnight! Remember what Ezra said? He said nobody goes in the tower at night."

"It certainly *is* strange," Henry agreed. "But it can't be a ghost. I'm sure there's a simple explanation and we'll find out in the morning."

Benny looked out the window again. "But — " he began. "Oh, all right," Benny said, getting slowly into his own bed.

Soon Benny was asleep, but Henry lay awake a little longer. *There couldn't possibly be anything wrong in the clock tower*, he thought. But he wasn't so sure.

The next day, the Aldens woke up early, excited about exploring the university. As they walked to the dining hall for breakfast,

Benny told the others about what he'd seen the night before.

"It was definitely a ghost," Benny said.

Henry grinned. "Probably not, although it did seem pretty strange that someone would be up there so late at night."

"Well, I'm sure there's a simple explanation," Grandfather assured them.

"That's just what I said," Henry told them.

After a hearty breakfast of juice, milk, and blueberry pancakes with syrup, Grandfather turned to Jessie, who was holding the schedule of reunion activities. "What looks good for this morning?" he asked.

"Let's see," she said, scanning down the page. She read aloud, " 'Saturday morning. Take a tour of the campus. See what's changed and what's the same. Meet at the base of the clock tower at ten A.M.' "

"That sounds interesting," said Violet.

Grandfather looked at his watch. "It's quarter to ten now."

"Let's go!" said Henry.

They were just approaching the clock tower when Violet spotted a familiar face. "Isn't that Ezra Stewart?" she asked. They walked over to say hello.

"Hello, Alden family. And what are you doing on this beautiful sunny day?" Ezra asked. He was as sharply dressed as he'd been the day before. Today he wore red-and-white suspenders with the Goldwin insignia on them. The children could guess that he appreciated school spirit.

"We're going on a tour of the campus," Jessie said.

"Doesn't that sound delightful," Ezra commented.

"I have a question for you," Benny said.

Ezra smiled down at Benny. "Fire away! Goldwin University trivia is my specialty."

"Last night, in the middle of the night, I saw a light on in the clock tower," Benny said. "Is someone up there at night?"

The smile on Ezra's face disappeared. "No, of course there isn't anyone up there at night," he said angrily. "Why would you think that?"

Benny seemed hurt by Ezra's tone. "Well, it's just that I saw a light — "

"You must have been mistaken," Ezra snapped. "Maybe you were dreaming."

"I saw it, too," Henry pointed out.

Ezra turned to Henry. "Then you must have been mistaken as well," he repeated.

"Is the tower locked at night?" Jessie asked.

"Well, no, I don't lock it, but I told you — nobody goes up there at night," Ezra said. "Now excuse me, but I must be going." He hurried off.

"My goodness, he certainly seemed upset, didn't he?" said Jessie.

"But he was so nice at first," said Benny sadly.

Violet spoke up. "It's like yesterday, when he started talking about his assistant, Andrea Barton. All of a sudden his whole mood changed."

"I guess he didn't like the idea that someone was up there who shouldn't be," Grandfather said.

"But don't you see?" Benny said, suddenly getting excited. "If Ezra says that no one goes up there at night, then there's only one explanation."

"And what might that be?" Jessie asked.

"It's a ghost! I told you!" Benny insisted.

"Oh, Benny," Henry said. "You know there's no such thing as ghosts."

"Are you sure?" Benny asked.

"Yes," said Grandfather. "Maybe Ezra is right, you were mistaken about the light. Maybe it was just a reflection from somewhere else."

"Or maybe someone is going up there who shouldn't be," said Henry.

Before the Aldens could discuss this possibility further, they heard a loud voice. "Good morning, Aldens!"

The family turned to see Joel and Don Dixon coming up the hill to join them. "Ready for the tour?"

"We sure are," said Grandfather.

Just then a blond man in a red Goldwin University T-shirt called out, "The tour is going to be starting now." The Dixons and Aldens walked toward him. A small group of people gathered around. "My name is Ethan, and I'll be your guide," the man said. "Some of the buildings you may remember, but a lot have been built since you graduated. You'll see they're working on a brand-new building right here on the Quad." He motioned behind him. "I'm sure you all remember the clock tower."

People nodded and smiled. "Hasn't changed a bit," one woman pointed out.

"When was the tower built?" asked Don.

"Around 1860. It's one of the oldest buildings here," Ethan said.

"Did it always have a carillon?" Don asked.

"Yes," said Ethan. "At the beginning, there were twenty-five bells. Over the years, more and more bells were donated to the school by generous alumni. Now there are forty-nine.

"We'll end our tour back here in time for the midday concert," Ethan continued. "Now, if you'll follow me, let's head on over this way, to the new science buildings."

"How old is the clock?" Don asked.

Ethan turned around. "You have a lot of good questions," he remarked. "It's the original clock — from 1860," Ethan said.

Don nodded.

"If there are no more questions, we'll move on," Ethan said, looking around at the group.

Joel and Grandfather were very impressed with the new science buildings, which were very tall and faced with glass. "They look a lot fancier than the old labs we had our classes in," Joel remarked. "Very modern buildings, don't you think, Don?"

Don seemed lost in his own thoughts.

"Don?" Joel asked after a moment.

"I'm sorry, Dad. What did you say?" asked Don.

"I was just noticing how modern these buildings are compared to the rest of the campus," said Joel.

"What? Oh, yes," Don said. But he didn't really seem to be paying attention.

A moment later, Ethan had led the tour to a group of very old-looking dormitories. "A Civil War battle was fought not far from here, and troops were housed in some of these buildings."

"What's the Civil War?" asked Benny.

"That was a war fought between the northern and southern parts of our country," said Grandfather. "It happened a long time ago, in the 1860s."

"Really? There was a war in the United States?" asked Benny.

"Yes, and lots of young men and boys left their families to go and fight," Grandfather said. "Many people were killed, or lost their homes and all their money. It was a terrible war."

The tour continued past many more interesting buildings and a large statue of James Goldwin, founder of the college. Finally they found themselves back at the clock tower.

"We'll go up to the top of the tower now, for anyone who wants to see the view," Ethan said.

"Great," said several people in the crowd as they headed into the tower and started up the steep, winding staircase. The Aldens followed, even though they'd already seen the view the day before. Ethan pointed out several more sights from the top of the tower. When he was finished, he said, "And that concludes our tour. Thanks so much for joining me."

"Thank you," said Jessie, and others on the tour echoed her.

The Aldens waited as the rest of the group headed back down the stairs. Just as they were getting ready to leave, a young woman came hurrying up the stairs. She was wearing blue jeans, clogs, and a bulky red sweatshirt with the word GOLDWIN stitched across the front in large white letters. Her long brown hair was pulled back in a ponytail that bounced as she walked.

"Hello!" Benny said as she entered the tower room. "You missed the tour, but I can tell you what we saw."

"Thanks," the woman said with a big smile, "but I go to school here. I probably could have given the tour."

"I bet you don't know all the stuff about the carillon," Benny said.

"I bet I do," the woman said, her smile growing larger. "I'm the assistant carillon player."

"You are?" Violet said. She remembered how upset Ezra had been when he talked about his assistant. This young woman seemed nice and friendly. How could she make him so angry?

"You must be Andrea Barton," Henry said.

"That's right. But you can call me Andi — all my friends do. How did you know my name?" Andrea asked.

"We met Ezra yesterday," Jessie said. "He told us all about the carillon, and we watched him play a concert."

"Pretty cool, isn't it?" Andrea said. "I'm giving the concert at noon. I came a little early to get ready." She looked around at the stacks of papers everywhere. She lifted a few piles and frowned.

"What are you looking for?" asked Henry.

"My glasses," Andi said. "I'm sure I left them here. And the other day I bought some new pieces of music to try out, and they disappeared, too. Then again, I'm not sure Ezra liked the idea of new music anyway." Andi opened a few drawers in the desk and looked inside. "It's almost as if there's a ghost in here, moving my things around!"

Benny's face lit up. "See? I told you there was a ghost," he said to his brother and sisters.

Andi laughed.

"Here are some glasses," Jessie said, picking up a pair that was lying on the windowsill. She handed them to Andi.

"Those aren't mine," Andi said. "They look like they belong to someone older. See, they have a little line in the middle of the glass. That means they're bifocals."

"Like mine," Grandfather said, taking off his glasses and cleaning them with his handkerchief. "The top part helps you see far away, and the bottom part helps you see close up."

"Maybe they belong to Ezra," Violet suggested.

"No," Andi said. "He doesn't wear glasses."

"Maybe someone on the tour left them," Jessie suggested.

"I don't remember anyone wearing glasses," said Henry.

"I bet they belong to the ghost!" said Benny.

"Benny thinks the clock tower is haunted," Henry explained. "He saw a light moving around up here late last night."

"Late last night?" Andi repeated. Then she laughed quickly. "Who would be up here in the middle of the night?"

"That's just what we were wondering," Jessie said. "We asked Ezra, and he said no one is supposed to be in here after the evening concert."

"That's right. I come up in between concerts a lot to practice," Andi said. "But not in the middle of the night, of course." She laughed again, a little nervously.

"That's why I think it's a ghost. A ghost who doesn't see very well, I guess." Benny waved the glasses.

"I guess not." Andi grinned at Benny. Then her face grew serious again, and she began shuffling through the papers some more. "And now I really do have to get ready for my concert."

"We'll go downstairs and listen from the Quad," Grandfather suggested. He had noticed that Andi seemed nervous. "I'm sure it's not easy to play with all of us standing right here."

Back down on the ground, the Aldens bought sandwiches and drinks at a small lunch stand set up next to the Quad. As they ate their picnic lunch, they listened to Andi's concert.

"I guess she found her music," Jessie said.

"Her music is a lot jazzier than Ezra's was," said Violet.

"Hey, I know this song," Henry pointed out. "It's a pop song. I heard it on the radio yesterday as we were driving."

"That's neat that she can play it on the carillon," Violet said.

"Ezra's stuff was good, too, but it was more classical music," Jessie remarked.

When the concert ended, Violet turned to the others. "She's a really great player. I wonder why she was so nervous."

"She was probably just excited about her concert," Jessie assured her sister. But privately she wondered whether something was bothering Andi, and whether it had anything to do with the light Benny had seen up in the tower.

CHAPTER 4

Do Ghosts Wear Sneakers?

That night, Henry and Benny were getting ready for bed. They both had their pajamas on and their teeth brushed. They were just climbing into their beds when Benny suddenly jumped back out.

"What are you doing?" Henry asked.

"Getting this," Benny explained, pulling his little alarm clock out of his suitcase.

"You don't need that," Henry said. "Grandfather told us we could sleep in tomorrow morning."

"It's not for tomorrow morning," Benny

said. "I'm setting it for midnight so I can see if the ghost is in the clock tower again."

"Benny!" Henry cried, throwing a pillow at his little brother. "Oh . . . all right."

But a few hours later, Henry wished he'd never agreed. A bell was ringing in his ears, and there was no sign of Benny turning it off.

"Benny! Benny!" Henry called out. "Turn off the alarm!" At last Henry sat up and looked over at Benny's bed. Benny was snuggled down under his covers, sound asleep.

"Oh, sure, you're going to get up," Henry muttered as he reached over to turn off the alarm. He had forgotten what a sound sleeper Benny was. Benny hadn't even heard the alarm.

But Henry had to smile, remembering how excited Benny had been to find out if the "ghost" would be back at midnight. "I won't even wake him," Henry said softly to himself. "I'll just take a quick look and then go back to sleep. I'm sure there's no one up there tonight."

Henry turned to the window. It was raining out. There was the clock tower, the clock shining brightly. And the window of the tower room was dark, just as it should be. Or was it?

Henry took a step closer to the window. He thought he'd seen something. But he must be imagining things. No — there it was again. A small light was flickering in the window.

"What is that?" Henry muttered to himself. He stepped right up to the window and watched as the light bounced around in the tower room. Then he rushed back over to Benny's bed and began shaking him.

"Benny, Benny! Wake up!" Henry cried.

It took Benny a few seconds to wake up and figure out where he was. "Henry?" he asked, rubbing his eyes. "What's going on?"

"Benny, hurry up! Come look!" Henry cried, pulling Benny to his feet. "There's a light in the tower!"

"There is?" Benny asked. He ran to the window and the two boys stood side by side in the dark room, looking up at the tower.

"Wow!" Benny said. "Someone's up there."

"But I don't think it's the same person as last night," Henry said.

"How do you know?" Benny asked.

"Because last night, the whole room was lit," Henry explained. "But tonight, it's just a little light bouncing around — like someone's carrying a flashlight."

"You're right!" Benny said. "Let's go wake the others."

A moment later, Jessie and Violet were standing beside their brothers looking up at the tower.

"Why would someone be up there with a flashlight on?" Jessie asked. "Why not just turn on the light?"

"I don't know," said Henry. "Unless this person doesn't want anyone to know he — or she — is there."

After several minutes, the light went out. The Aldens waited a few more minutes before agreeing that whoever had been up there must have left.

"Can we go back to sleep now?" Violet asked, yawning.

"Yes, definitely," said Henry.

"But what about our ghost?" Benny asked.

"First of all, it's *not* a ghost," Jessie said.

"How do you know?" Benny demanded.

"Well, aside from the fact that there's no such thing as ghosts, a ghost certainly wouldn't need to carry a flashlight," Jessie pointed out.

"Yeah, I guess you're right," Benny said. He sounded disappointed. "So who is it, then?"

"I don't know," said Jessie. Then she yawned. "But I'm tired. We'll figure it out in the morning."

The next morning the Aldens were awakened by the sound of the bells playing outside. But something was wrong.

"The song sounds awful!" Violet said.

"I wonder what's wrong," Jessie said.

A moment later the music stopped, right in the middle. There was a strange, sudden silence. Jessie and Violet quickly got dressed and joined their brothers in the small kitchenette.

"What happened to the bells?" Benny asked.

"I don't know," said Jessie. "The song sounded all wrong."

The children made some breakfast with the groceries they'd bought the day before — scrambled eggs, toast and jam, orange juice, and a cup of coffee for Grandfather. Just as everything was ready, Grandfather came out of the bathroom, freshly showered and shaved.

"Something smells good," Grandfather said.

"We made breakfast," Jessie said. "Come and have some."

As the Aldens sat down to eat, they told Grandfather about the carillon. He hadn't heard it because he'd been in the shower.

"It sounded fine last night," Grandfather said.

"Maybe whoever was up there last night did something to it," Benny said.

"Someone was up there last night?" Mr. Alden asked.

The children told him what they'd seen at midnight.

"I think we should go up there this morning and investigate," said Benny.

"You go ahead," said Grandfather. "I'll just relax with my coffee and read the paper. But be back here by noon. There's a picnic this afternoon that should be a lot of fun."

"Okay, Grandfather," Jessie called as they left.

Half an hour later, the Aldens were climbing the hill to the tower.

"It sure is muddy," Violet pointed out.

"It rained pretty hard last night," Henry said. "Be careful you don't slip."

When they got up to the tower room, Ezra was there, a toolbox in his hands. He was not in a good mood. "Did you hear the bells this morning?" he asked when he saw the Aldens.

"Yes," said Violet. "What happened to them?"

Ezra shook his head. "I'm not sure, but the whole carillon is a mess. Somehow, several of the wires and springs were broken, and some of the clappers were loosened.

Look." The children looked where Ezra was pointing. Just as he had said, several wires seemed to have been snapped, so they no longer went all the way down into the carillon.

"When I tried to play my usual morning piece, several bells weren't ringing when they were supposed to," said Ezra. "When I realized what was happening, I stopped and went to get my toolbox. I've been trying to fix the carillon and the bells ever since."

"This couldn't have just happened by accident, could it?" Henry asked.

"I bet it has something to do with the person who was up here last night," said Benny.

Ezra stopped what he was doing and looked up. "What person?"

"We don't exactly know," said Benny.

"What Benny means is, we saw a light up here last night," Jessie explained.

"We think someone was in here, carrying a flashlight," added Henry.

"Maybe that person broke the bells," Benny said.

"You saw a light?" Ezra said.

"Yes," said Benny.

Ezra frowned for a moment. "Did you see anything else besides the light?"

"No," said Jessie.

"Listen," Ezra said gruffly. "I get up very early to do the morning concert. I come up with my coffee and my paper before the sun's even up. Now, if you'll excuse me, I've got to go back to my house — my small screwdriver isn't in here. I must have left it at home. I'll be back in a little while."

Ezra had just left when suddenly Violet spotted something.

On the floor beside the practice carillon was a muddy footprint. Violet turned to Benny. "Do ghosts wear sneakers?" she asked, pointing.

"Hey! Look at that!" Henry cried. Jessie hurried over to look at the footprint.

"This wasn't here yesterday, was it?" Jessie asked.

"No — we would have noticed it," said Violet.

"And it just started raining last night, so there wasn't any mud yesterday," said Henry. "Whoever left this must have been here since last night."

"It probably wasn't Ezra," said Henry. "He wears loafers, and they have smooth soles."

"What kind of shoes does Andi wear?" Benny asked.

"When we met her she had on clogs," said Violet. "I remember because I thought they looked so comfortable."

"Do you think the person who left this print is the same person who broke the carillon?" Jessie asked.

"I don't know," said Henry. "It could be."

"And don't forget those glasses we found," said Violet. "Someone left those up here, too."

"I knew we'd get another mystery to solve!" said Benny. And he broke into a big grin.

CHAPTER 5

Buried Treasure!

The Aldens headed back to their dormitory, still talking about the footprint.

The Aldens' suite was empty, but the children heard voices from next door. They knocked on the Dixons' suite and found Grandfather and Joel sitting in the living room, drinking coffee and chatting.

"Come join us," Grandfather said.

"Have a doughnut," Joel offered, motioning to the box on the small kitchen table.

"Thanks," said Jessie as she and the others each took a powdery sugar doughnut.

The two men went back to their conversation as the children sat down at the kitchen table and ate.

"Look, here's Don's old book about Goldwin," Violet said, spotting the book with the cracked leather cover lying on the kitchen counter.

"I bet it has some neat old pictures," said Jessie. "Joel, is it okay if we look at Don's book?"

"Sure," Joel replied.

As Benny reached for the book, Jessie quickly added, "First we need to wash our hands."

The children washed the powdered sugar off their fingers and dried their hands carefully. Then Violet picked up the book and put it in the center of the table. Everyone gathered around as she turned the pages one by one.

"Look at this old picture of the campus," said Henry, pointing to a brown-tinted photograph. "There are only a few buildings here."

"And here's one that shows them building the clock tower," said Benny.

"Wow," said Jessie. "It says underneath that from the top of the tower you can see all the way to Buttermilk Falls. We'll have to look for that next time we're up there."

"Hey, look, there's a chapter called 'The Secrets of Goldwin University,' " said Henry.

"Secrets?" said Benny. "What secrets?"

Henry began to read a little bit of the chapter. "It says there are many secret hidden places on campus. And there are rumors of a treasure buried here!"

"A treasure!" the others repeated.

"I'd like to see that," said Benny.

Just then the door opened and Don came in. "Hello," he called out.

"Have a nice walk?" Joel asked him.

"Sure did," said Don. "I walked by the river, all the way up to the waterfalls and back."

"We were just having some coffee and

doughnuts," said Mr. Alden. "Come join us."

"Don't mind if I do," said Don, going into the kitchen area to get himself some coffee. "What have you kids been up to?"

"Not much," said Jessie. "We were just looking at this old book of yours. I hope you don't mind."

"No, not at all," said Don, pouring himself a cup of coffee. Suddenly he turned around. "Wait a minute — what book?"

"This one," said Violet, holding it up. "The one about Goldwin."

Don put down his coffee cup and grabbed the book out of Violet's hands. "Where did you find this?" he demanded.

"It was right here in the kitchen," Henry said.

"We were being really careful with it," said Jessie. "We made sure our hands were clean."

Don turned a few pages, as if making sure the book was still in one piece. "This is a very old, delicate book," he said angrily. "It's not something to play with."

"But we weren't playing — " said Benny.

But it was too late. Don had taken the book and strode quickly out of the room. A moment later he was back, empty-handed. "I'm sorry, but that book is very . . . special to me. I wouldn't want anything to happen to it." He picked up his coffee cup and walked into the living room to sit down with the two men.

The children just looked at one another quietly, wondering about Don's sudden anger. Why would he get so upset over a book?

A short while later, it was time to go to the picnic. It was being held on the Quad, and there were tables and tables piled with food: fried chicken, all different kinds of salads, rolls, pickles, and watermelon and cupcakes for dessert. The Aldens and the Dixons each helped themselves to a plateful of food and then sat down in the shade to enjoy it. When he'd finished his first plateful, Benny went back two more times to get more of the delicious potato salad and extra slices of watermelon.

At the end of the lively afternoon, the Aldens walked into town and had dinner at the Chariot, one of Grandfather's favorite pizza places. "We used to come here all the time when I was a student," he told them.

"I can't believe it's still here," said Jessie.

"Wait till you taste the pizza. Then you'll believe it," Mr. Alden assured her.

The pizza was just as good as Grandfather had promised. After dinner, the Aldens took a stroll through town. Grandfather couldn't believe all the large buildings that had been built since he was there last.

When they finally returned to their suite, the children were worn out.

"I'm ready for bed," said Benny. "I'm not even going to set the alarm tonight."

"Good!" said Henry. "I could use a good night's sleep."

The next morning, the Aldens awoke feeling rested and ready for another busy day of activities.

"There's a concert this afternoon that Joel and I are going to," said Grandfather, "but I think I'm just going to relax in the room this morning. What do you kids plan to do?"

"I want to look for the treasure," said Benny.

"Treasure?" asked Grandfather.

Jessie told him what they'd read the day before in Don's book.

"I was here for four years and I never saw any treasure," Mr. Alden said with a chuckle. "But enjoy yourselves. Meet me back here for lunch."

"Remember the book also said that from the top of the clock tower you can see all the way to the waterfalls," said Jessie.

"That's right," Violet recalled. "Let's go up and see if you really can. It's a clear day."

Once again, the Aldens found themselves climbing to the top of the tower. "Our leg muscles are getting a good workout here," said Henry.

"They sure are," Violet agreed.

The top of the tower was dark and quiet today. The morning concert had ended a short while ago, and no one was up there.

"Now, what did it say in the book?" Henry asked.

"If you look out the west window you can see Buttermilk Falls," Jessie reminded him.

"How do we know which window faces west?" asked Benny.

"The sun came up over there," said Violet. "So that's the east."

"Then that's the west," Jessie said, pointing to the opposite window.

The children all went to that window and looked out.

"Look, there are the falls!" Henry said, pointing off in the distance.

"I see people climbing on the rocks," Jessie said.

"Hey, let me see," said Benny.

Jessie moved aside to give Benny room to look out. As she turned away from the window, she noticed a folded piece of paper on the floor in the corner. "What's that?" she mumbled to herself. She went over and picked up the piece of paper. It was yellowed and felt strange — crumbly and rough, as if it were very old. Jessie carefully unfolded the paper and was surprised by the fancy writing on it.

"You guys!" she said. "Look at this!"

The other children turned around to see what Jessie was holding.

"What have you got?" Violet asked.

"A letter," Jessie said. "Only it's really old. I found it in the corner."

The others crowded around.

"There's a seal at the top," Henry said, pointing to a circle design that had been pressed into the top of the paper. "It says, 'Goldwin University, Office of the President.'"

"What does that mean?" asked Benny. "Is this from the President of the United States?"

"No, it's from the president of this college," Jessie explained. "The president at a university is sort of like the principal at your school. This is his or her stationery."

"It says 'May 5, 1863' in the corner," Violet pointed out. "This letter is really old — it was written over a hundred years ago!"

"Wow!" said Benny.

"That's even older than Grandfather," Violet pointed out.

"So what does it say?" Benny asked. "The writing looks really strange."

"They didn't have ballpoint pens back then," Jessie said. "They had to dip their pens in ink to write. And people had very fancy handwriting."

"They sure did," said Benny. "I can't even read it." He had just learned to read and had enough trouble with regular printing.

"This is what it says," said Jessie, reading aloud:

Dear Aaron,

I have hidden our gold and silver so the army shall not get it. Do not be concerned — it shall be safe until you come home from the war, and only then shall we dig it up. Should anything happen to me, I give you this clue to where it lies hidden:

Listen to the music and take one hundred sixty-one steps. Remember, the key to the problem is right before the face.

Your loving father

When Jessie had finished reading, she looked up to see her sister and two brothers all standing openmouthed, staring at her.

"I don't believe it!" said Violet.

"There really is a treasure buried here!" said Henry.

"I knew it! I knew it!" said Benny.

"Wait a minute," Jessie said. "Let's think about this before we go and get all excited. We don't even know if this letter is real!"

"It looks real," said Benny.

"It certainly does," Violet had to agree, fingering the embossed seal of the president's office. "I mean, look at this crumbling old paper. And people just don't write like this anymore."

"But where did the letter come from?" asked Henry. "We've been up here several times in the last few days, and this is the first time we've seen it."

"You're right," Violet agreed. "Someone must have just dropped this here recently."

"Do you think the person who dropped

it was hunting for the treasure?" Benny asked.

"Could be," said Henry.

"What do you think we should do, Jessie?" Violet asked.

Jessie had been silently staring out the window. Suddenly she turned around. "I know how we can find out if this letter is real."

"How?" asked Violet.

"The library is right down there." Jessie pointed out the window. "Let's go there and look up some information about the history of Goldwin University."

"Great idea," Henry said.

Jessie folded the letter carefully and the four children hurried down the narrow staircase, going as quickly as they could on the twisting stone steps.

A few minutes later, the Aldens were at the front desk of Goldwin's main library. The librarian there was tall and thin with short brown hair. "Hello, I'm Mrs. Brooke. Can I help you?" she asked.

"We're looking for a book that has information about the history of the college," said Jessie.

"Just a minute," Mrs. Brooke said. She came back a moment later with a thick, heavy book. The cover read, *Goldwin University: From Past to Present.* "This book has a lot of information."

"Thanks," said Henry, picking up the large book and walking over to a table by a window. The others followed. He set the book down and opened it to the table of contents. The children studied the page for a moment.

"This sounds like a good place to look," Henry said, pointing to a chapter titled "Presidents of the University." "It starts on page fifty-six."

Jessie flipped to that page. She read aloud from the first page, " 'The university was founded in 1860 and the first president was named Joshua Chambers. He held the office until 1864.' "

"This letter was written in 1863," said Violet. "So he must be the one who wrote it."

"Look, there's a picture," Benny pointed out. "Is that him?"

Jessie looked at the black-and-white picture of a handsome man with dark hair and small round glasses. Underneath the photograph it said, *Joshua Chambers, First President of Goldwin University*. "Yes, Benny, that's him."

The children studied the photograph for a moment.

"Let's see what else it says about him," Jessie suggested. She quickly read the page to herself. Suddenly her eyes widened and she gasped.

"What is it?" Benny asked. "Tell us!"

"He's the one who wrote the letter," said Jessie.

"How do you know?" Henry asked.

"It says that he had a son named Aaron who served in the army during the Civil War," Jessie told them.

"And this letter is addressed to someone named Aaron, from his father," said Violet.

Jessie continued reading. Suddenly she said, "Oh, how terrible!"

"What?" the other three cried.

Jessie explained, "It says that Chambers died in 1864, while his son was off at war — and Aaron was killed in battle a few months later."

"How sad," Violet said.

"He died the year after he wrote the letter," Benny said.

The children were silent for a moment. They gazed at the picture of the kind-looking man and thought about how sad his story was.

All of a sudden Henry said, "Do you realize what this means? President Chambers died before he got to show his son where the treasure was."

"But remember, there were some clues in the letter," Benny said.

"I wonder if Aaron figured them out," Violet said.

"He might not have had a chance," said Henry. "It says he was killed in a battle just a short time after his father died."

"Then that means . . ." Jessie began.

"The treasure is still buried!" Benny whispered.

CHAPTER 6

Going on a Treasure Hunt

"Now, just wait a minute, Benny," Henry said. "Someone might already have found the treasure, you know. I mean, we're not the first ones to have seen this letter."

"No, we're not," Jessie agreed. "I wonder who found it first and who left it in the tower."

"Even if we're not the first, we can still look for the treasure, can't we?" Benny asked.

"Yes, we certainly can," said Henry.

"Let's take a look at what it says in the letter again," suggested Jessie. "But first I'm going to return this book to Mrs. Brooke."

While Jessie took the book back to the librarian, Violet laid the letter on top of the table and carefully unfolded it.

"What does the clue say again?" Benny asked.

Violet read, "It says, 'Listen to the music and take one hundred sixty-one steps. Remember, the key to the problem is right in front of the face.' "

"What do you think he meant by 'listen to the music'?" asked Jessie, who had just come back.

"They definitely didn't have radios or CDs back then," said Henry with a laugh.

As they were talking, the silence of the library was broken by the sound of the bells.

"The midday concert!" Violet cried.

"I know, can you believe it's already lunchtime?" Jessie asked.

"And it sounds like Ezra fixed the carillon," Henry added.

"No, I mean, that's the music you listen

to here at Goldwin," Violet said excitedly. "The music Joshua Chambers was talking about!"

"You're right!" Jessie said. "Good thinking, Violet."

"Did the carillon play way back then?" Henry asked.

"Yes," Jessie said. "On the tour they said it was put in when the tower was first built. That was in 1860."

"Okay, so we've figured out the first part of the clue," said Henry. "Now what about the rest of it?"

"Read the second part again," Benny said.

Violet read, " 'Take one hundred sixty-one steps — ' "

"I know!" Benny shouted all of a sudden. "That's how many steps it is to the top of the clock tower. Remember, Mr. Stewart told us that the first day we met him?"

"Great job, Benny!" said Jessie.

"You have a good memory," Henry added.

"So President Chambers was telling his son to go to the top of the tower," Violet said.

"Then why are we still sitting here?" Benny asked. "Let's go!"

The children hurried out of the library and walked as quickly as they could up the winding tower stairs.

At the top, they found Ezra playing the carillon. He gave the children a smile as they came in. He seemed to have fixed all the broken wires. The children looked around the room, wondering where the treasure might be hidden.

When Ezra had finished playing, he turned to the children. "What brings you all back here again?"

"We're on a treasure hunt!" Benny said.

"A treasure hunt?" Ezra repeated. "Oh, I see. Why are you looking up here? Nothing here but a bunch of old music books. And the carillon, of course."

"I see you've fixed it," Henry said.

"Yes, I did," Ezra said. "It took me all morning. But I think it sounds okay now."

"It sounded good to me," said Violet.

Jessie showed Ezra the old letter. "This is why we're on a treasure hunt," she explained. "We found this up here after you left."

Ezra took the letter Jessie was holding. "This looks very old! Wherever did you find it?"

"Right here, in the corner," Benny said.

"I wonder how it got there," Ezra said. He read the letter and handed it back to Violet. "I can't believe I wouldn't notice something like this."

"We figured out that the letter was from President Joshua Chambers," Jessie said. "And it seems he was telling his son to come up here to the clock tower."

"Well, as I said, there's no treasure up here. I've been here long enough to know that." Ezra went over to his desk and put away the music he'd just played.

Jessie took another look at the letter. "What do you think he means by the 'key to the problem'?"

The children all thought about that for a moment. They looked around at the old photos on the walls.

Just then the bells played four loud notes, startling the children.

"What was that?" asked Benny.

"That means it's quarter to one," Ezra said. "The bells are programmed to ring the hours, quarter hours, and half hours by themselves. The bells aren't just for music; they also work with the clock."

All of a sudden Henry said, "Hey! Maybe that's it."

"What's it?" asked Jessie.

"I have an idea about what Chambers meant when he said the answer is 'right before the face,' " Henry said. "Look up there!" He pointed to a large round door over the west-facing window. "That's the back of the clock, right, Ezra?"

"Yes, it is," Ezra said. "I open that door to fix the clock or reset it."

"Think about what you call the front of a clock," Henry said.

"You mean its face?" Jessie asked. Then her face lit up. "Oh, I get it!"

"Maybe President Chambers wasn't talking about a person's face," Henry explained to the others. "Maybe he was talking about the clock's face."

"You mean that somehow the 'key' is in the clock's face?" Benny asked.

"I guess so," Henry said.

"Ezra, is that possible?" asked Jessie. "Could there be something hidden in the clock's face?"

"I don't see how," Ezra said. "I clean that clock once a month. I'd see anything hidden there."

"Yes, you would," Henry agreed.

"Could you open up the clock now?" Jessie asked. "Maybe there's something in there you never noticed."

"I love to show people how that big old clock works. It's pretty amazing," Ezra said. He went to a cabinet on the wall and took out a small key. Then he pulled a stepladder out from under his desk and placed it under the clock. He got up on the ladder and unlocked the back of the clock. The large round door swung open, revealing the inside of the giant clock.

"Wow, look at that," Benny said, staring

at all the gears turning inside the clock. "That's cool."

Ezra gave a quick explanation of how the old clock worked and how he took care of it. "If each of you would like to come up, one at a time, you can take a closer look."

The children took turns stepping up on the ladder and studying the inside of the clock — first Benny, then Violet, then Jessie, and finally Henry.

"Could something have been hidden inside the back here?" Henry asked when it was his turn.

"I can't imagine — I'm sure I'd have seen it by now," Ezra said. "I have to take apart all the machinery to clean it."

"I was so sure there would be something in the clock," Henry said. He was disappointed.

"Can I look again?" Benny asked. He didn't want to give up the treasure hunt yet.

"Go ahead," Ezra said. "But I'm *sure* there's nothing hidden in there."

Henry stepped down from the ladder and Benny stepped back up. He looked all around the clock, trying to think of a place Ezra might never have looked. He noticed a tiny crevice around the rim of the clock, where it attached to the wall. Benny slipped his small fingers in there and felt around. "Hey! There's something in here!" he cried suddenly.

"There is?" Ezra asked.

"Yes, it feels like a little lump of crumbly stuff — paper, maybe," Benny said. "I just can't quite get my fingers around it."

"Maybe there's something in my toolbox that will help," Ezra said.

"I'll look," Jessie offered, going to get Ezra's toolbox from his desk. After a moment she said, "How about these needle-nosed pliers?"

"That ought to work," Ezra said. Jessie handed them to him.

Ezra stepped up next to Benny. He poked the long, thin pliers down into the crevice where Benny had felt something. "I've got it — whatever it is," he said. Slowly, he pulled out a small bundle of crumbling brown paper.

"It's a little package," Benny said. "And it looks really old."

Ezra handed the package to Henry as Benny stepped back down the ladder. Ezra closed and locked the clock door. Then he joined the Aldens, who were clustered around his desk. Henry was carefully opening the flat brown package.

"There's a key," he said.

"The 'key to the problem,'" Jessie said with a smile.

"And a note," Henry added. He slowly unwrapped the note and read it aloud.

Aaron —

If you have found this key, then you must have figured out my first note. Good work.

On a warm summer's morn when the clock strikes six, set yourself between North and South. The tower will point the way.

Your father

"Another clue!" Benny said.

"I wonder what it means," Violet said.

"I can't believe it!" Ezra said. "Well, this

has certainly been excitement enough for one morning. I'm ready to go home and have my lunch."

"Lunch — that's right," Jessie said. "We were supposed to meet Grandfather back at the suite at lunchtime, remember?"

"May we take this key and note with us, Ezra?" Henry asked.

Ezra paused. "Well, you did find them," he said, "so I guess that would only be fair."

"We'd better go, then," Jessie said. "Thanks for opening the clock for us!"

"My pleasure," Ezra said.

"We'll see you later!" Benny called over his shoulder as he and the other Aldens hurried down the stairs.

Back at the suite, Grandfather was just putting his plate and cup in the sink. "Here you are!" he said. "I thought you weren't coming. I went ahead and ate without you."

"Sorry we're so late — " Jessie began.

"But wait until you hear about our treasure hunt!" Benny cut in excitedly.

The Aldens told their grandfather all

about what they'd found. When at last they'd finished their story, Grandfather sat looking at the two old letters and the key. "That's amazing!" he said. "So there really is a treasure buried here."

"But how do we find it?" Violet asked.

"I don't know, but I'm sure you will," Grandfather said.

"Can we eat first?" Benny asked. "I'm starving."

"It is way past lunchtime," Jessie said. "It's nearly two o'clock."

"Is it that late?" Grandfather asked. "I'm joining Joel for a concert. It starts at two. I told him I'd meet him in Rhodes Hall, where they're giving the concert. I'd better get going. How about if we meet back here at dinnertime?"

"Sounds great!" Jessie said.

"Be careful with those letters," Grandfather said. "If they're really that old, they're valuable historical documents."

"We'll be very careful," Violet assured him.

"There's ham and cheese in the refrigerator," Grandfather reminded them. "And there's fruit, too. See you later!"

The children waved as Grandfather left. Then they made themselves lunch. They had been so busy treasure hunting, they hadn't realized how hungry they were.

After a few minutes Jessie said, "I've been wondering how that letter got into the tower in the first place."

"Me, too," said Violet.

"I think someone must have found it — somewhere — and figured out that it was talking about the clock tower, just like we did," said Henry.

"Then that person must have gone up to the tower to look, just like we did. And dropped the note while he or she was there," said Jessie.

"I bet it's the same person who was up there at night," said Violet, selecting a peach from the basket on the counter. "The person went up when he or she knew no one would be around."

"But why?" Benny asked, biting into a plum.

"Probably to keep the treasure and not share it," Jessie said. "But that would be wrong — the treasure belongs to the Chambers family."

"Let's take a look at that second note," Henry said.

As the other children cleared away the lunch dishes, Violet went to get the letters and key. She had placed them on the counter away from the food so they wouldn't get dirty.

When the table was cleared, Violet spread out the second letter. The children sat down to look at it.

"What's a 'morn'?" asked Benny.

"It means morning," Jessie explained. "What do you think he means by 'set yourself between North and South'?"

"I have no idea," said Henry. "It sounds as if he's talking about the Civil War again. That war pitted the North against the South."

"But what does that have to do with the treasure?" Benny wanted to know.

"How do you think the tower will point the way?" Violet asked. "It points straight up in the air."

The children all sat quietly for several minutes.

"I think we need help," Jessie said.

"Who could help us?" Henry wondered. "This time it's not as simple as going to the library."

"Remember Grandfather said Professor Meyer knew everything about Goldwin?" Violet recalled. "Maybe she could help us."

"That's a good idea," Henry said. "She must have an office here on campus. Let's go find it."

"I bet it's in McGraw Hall," said Jessie. "On our tour they said that was where the history classes were, and Professor Meyer is a history professor."

The Aldens left their suite and headed up the hill to McGraw Hall. As they were cutting across the Quad, they saw Don Dixon heading toward them.

"Hi, Don!" Benny called out.

Don looked up, startled. He seemed lost in his own thoughts and very upset. "Oh, hello," he said distractedly.

"Is something the matter?" Violet asked.

"Something the matter? No, no," Don said. Then he paused. "Do you remember the other day when you were looking through that old book?"

"Yes," Jessie said.

"By any chance, did you notice . . ." Don stopped talking, and seemed to change his mind. "Oh, never mind."

"Are you sure — " Violet began, but Don cut her off.

"I've got to go." He rushed off down the hill.

The Aldens watched him walk away.

Jessie shrugged. "I wonder what's bugging him."

"Who knows?" said Henry.

"Come on, let's go find Professor Meyer," Benny reminded them.

CHAPTER 7

Guess Who's Coming to Dinner!

A few minutes later, the children were standing inside McGraw Hall, looking up at the directory on the wall.

"It says Professor Meyer's office is on the first floor," said Henry. "Room 106."

The children passed a large lecture hall and found Room 106 at the back of the building. Jessie knocked on the door.

"Come in," said a voice from inside.

Jessie opened the door and stepped in. Professor Meyer was standing next to a large, messy desk covered with papers. She was stuffing some of the papers into a large canvas bag that was already overflowing with papers and books. Again she was wearing a lively patterned dress with a brightly colored hat and matching sneakers.

"Well, if it isn't the Aldens," she said.

"Professor, we have a question for you," said Jessie.

"I hope it's a quick one," Professor Meyer said. "I was just on my way out."

"Actually, it's not a quick one," Jessie said. "Is there another time we could talk to you?"

"How about over dinner?" Henry suggested. "I'm sure our grandfather would enjoy chatting with you as well."

"What a lovely idea," the professor said. "I would invite you to my place, but I'm not much of a cook, I must confess. And my house is such a mess."

Looking around the cluttered office, the children had no trouble believing that.

"We'll make dinner for you at our suite," Jessie offered.

"Now, that would be a treat," Professor

Meyer said. "What time shall I come?"

"What time did Grandfather say he'd be home?" Henry asked.

"I think the concert ends at five," Jessie said. "How about six o'clock? We're in Sage Hall, Suite B-8."

"I will see you then," the professor said, picking up her overstuffed bag and putting it on her shoulder. The children stepped into the hallway with her. She shut and locked her office door.

"Where are you going now?" Benny piped up.

"Now? Oh, I'm going to, um . . . now, where *am* I going?" She paused for a moment. "Where did you say your grandfather was?"

"He's at a concert in Rhodes Hall," said Henry.

"Oh, yes, that's right. That's where I'm headed, too," Julia Meyer said.

"You know it started a while ago," Jessie said.

"Did it?" asked Ms. Meyer. "That's all right. I'll just be a little late. Good-bye!"

The children watched her walk away.

"That was sort of strange, wasn't it?" asked Henry. "It seemed as if she didn't know where she was going."

"She's a very unusual woman," said Jessie. "Now we'd better get to the store and figure out what we're going to make her for dinner."

A short while later, the Aldens were at the local grocery store, pushing their cart to the checkout counter. They had decided to make hamburgers, corn on the cob, and a green salad, and they had gotten ice cream for dessert. Just then, Jessie spotted Andrea Barton at the counter ahead of them. She was smiling and humming to herself.

"Hello again," Jessie said.

"Hello!" Andi said. Almost instantly her happy face grew serious. "Oh, um, I'm glad I ran into you," she said. Her voice sounded tense and nervous.

"So are we," Benny said. "Your concert the other day was great."

"Thanks," Andi said, a smile filling her face. But then she grew serious again. "I just wanted to ask you, um . . ."

"Yes?" Violet asked.

"Well, nothing really, just . . ." She twirled a piece of hair. "Please don't say anything to Ezra about what I said yesterday, okay?"

"Sure," said Jessie. After a moment she asked, "But what did you say?"

Andi laughed briefly. "Never mind," she said, picking up her bag of groceries. "I'll see you around."

The Aldens paid for their groceries and left the store. Their arms were loaded down with grocery bags.

"What do you think Andi meant when she asked us not to say anything to Ezra?" Violet asked as they walked.

"I was wondering that, too," said Jessie. "Was it that she told us she came in a lot to practice?"

"I thought it was about losing her glasses," said Benny.

"And losing the new music she bought,"

Henry added. "Remember she said Ezra probably wouldn't have liked it?"

"I wonder why she always seems so nervous," Violet said. "She's so nice and so talented. She should be happier."

When they got back to their suite, Jessie began shaping the ground beef into round patties. Henry and Violet washed and tore the lettuce and cut up carrots and tomatoes for the salad. Benny husked the corn and put a large pot of water on the stove. They would wait until dinnertime, when Grandfather came home, to boil the corn and fry the burgers. After the food was prepared, the children set the table and placed some flowers in the center.

"That looks nice," Violet said.

As they waited for Grandfather to arrive, the children got out a deck of cards and began to play.

"I can't stop thinking about the buried treasure," Jessie said as she shuffled the cards.

"Me neither!" said Benny, his eyes aglow.

"Do you think that someone we know is the person who's after it?" asked Henry.

"Like who?" said Violet.

"Oh, I don't know," Henry said. "But some of the people we've met here have acted, well, strangely. Like Ezra."

Jessie began to deal the cards. "You think he's the one who found the letter and started looking in the tower?"

"Could be," Henry said. "Maybe that's why he got so angry when we asked him if anyone goes up there at night — because *he's* going up there, and he doesn't want anyone to know."

"But he didn't seem to know about the treasure at all," said Violet. "In fact, he was surprised that we actually found something in the clock."

"Hmmm, that's true," Jessie said. "But he could have been pretending."

Henry agreed. "He helped us out — but maybe that was so he could find out for himself where the key was hidden."

"I've been wondering about Andi," said Violet, picking up her cards. "Ezra said everything was okay until she started working there. Maybe she took the job in the tower so she could look for the treasure."

"Go on," Jessie said thoughtfully.

Violet continued, "Remember that day she was searching for something and she said it was her glasses? Maybe it was really that letter that she'd misplaced, and then we found it not long afterward."

"And today in the grocery store she was certainly worried about something," said Jessie. "She seems to be keeping something secret from Ezra."

"And Ezra seems to be hiding something from us," said Benny. "Something about going up in the tower at night."

"But remember, whoever went up there broke the carillon," said Henry. "Why would Ezra do that?"

"That's true," said Benny.

"Don't forget the muddy footprint," Henry said. "Neither Ezra nor Andi seem to wear sneakers."

The children stopped talking and concentrated on their game of cards for a moment. After Jessie had taken her turn, she said, "Don Dixon has also been acting strangely. He got so upset about that old book, and we were being really careful with it. He still seemed upset about it today when we saw him on the Quad. Maybe he was afraid we'd read something about the treasure in there. And then on the tour he asked so many questions about the clock tower. I bet it's because he was trying to figure out where the treasure is hidden."

"But Don is Joel's son and Joel is Grandfather's good friend," Violet pointed out. "Do you really think he'd act so sneaky?"

Jessie shrugged. "I don't know. I really don't."

"Well, I do know one thing," Benny said, laying down his cards to show the others. "I won!"

A short while later, Grandfather returned from the concert. As he came in the door, he was humming lightly under his breath.

"How was the concert?" Violet asked.

"It was wonderful," Grandfather said. "It was a choral group, and they sang some lovely songs from when I was young.

Reminded me of your grandmother." He smiled fondly at the memory. "At the end, they sang the school's fight song and anthem."

"That sounds great," Jessie commented.

"How did your treasure hunt go?" Mr. Alden asked.

"We didn't get very far," Violet said. "We went to ask Professor Meyer for help, but she was busy."

"So we invited her for dinner tonight," Henry said. "I hope that's all right with you."

"Sure it is," Grandfather said. "I was just noticing how nicely you set the table. I was wondering if that was just for me."

"We went into town and bought some burgers and corn," Jessie said.

"She should be here soon," Violet added. "Did you see her at the concert? She said she was going."

"She was at the concert?" Grandfather thought for a moment. "I must have missed her. I'm surprised, though, because it wasn't a very large room."

"Hmmmm," said Henry, pulling Violet aside. "I wonder if she really was going to the concert, or if she just made that up when we told her Grandfather would be there. She didn't seem to know much about it."

"But why would she make it up?" asked Violet.

"I don't know. It might have something to do with her 'special project,' " said Henry.

Just then there was a knock at the door.

"That must be Professor Meyer now," Grandfather said, going to greet her.

"Hello," he said as he opened the door.

"Nice to see you, Jimmy," Professor Meyer said as she came into the suite. "Hello, children," she called. "How pretty the table looks!"

"Come sit down," Jessie said. "Dinner will be ready in a few minutes."

"Did you enjoy the concert?" Violet asked.

"The concert?" Professor Meyer looked puzzled.

Henry shot a look at the others as if to

say, *See? She didn't even go to the concert.*

But after a moment the professor said, "Oh, the concert! It was lovely."

"It was, wasn't it?" Grandfather agreed.

With help from Grandfather, the children fried the burgers, boiled the corn, and tossed the salad. Soon everything was ready.

"This all looks so good!" Professor Meyer said, sitting down to eat.

The food was delicious, and the conversation lively. Professor Meyer told them lots of good stories about the old days at Goldwin. It wasn't until they had finished eating that the children decided to bring up Joshua Chambers's letters.

As soon as the table was cleared, Henry said, "Professor Meyer, we wanted to ask you about a couple of old letters and a key we found."

"Oh, yes, you did have a question for me," she recalled.

Violet handed the letters to the professor. "Oh, how interesting," she said, carefully unfolding the yellowed papers. "Wherever did you find these?"

"Up in the clock tower," Benny said.

Professor Meyer had put the letters down on the table and was feeling around in her pockets for something. "Now, where did I . . ." she muttered to herself.

"Are you looking for something?" Henry asked.

"My glasses," she said.

"They're on top of your head," Benny said, trying to keep from laughing.

"They are?" she said. She put her hand up and touched them. "Oh, goodness, you're right!" She laughed heartily, and the others joined her. "Silly me!"

"I think those are the same glasses as Mrs. McGregor's — our housekeeper," said Benny.

"They are?" Grandfather asked.

"Yeah, I think so," Benny said. "They look so familiar."

"Let's see these letters," Professor Meyer said. She read the first letter quickly, and then turned to the second, and studied it as well. "So that's what happened to it," she said softly to herself.

"What did you say?" Benny asked.

"Oh, um, nothing," Professor Meyer said quickly.

The Aldens explained how they had found the first letter, and the research they had done in the library. "That was some good thinking," Professor Meyer said to Jessie. "The library is a wonderful resource. Maybe you'll be a professor one day. We spend a lot of time in the library looking things up."

Jessie blushed with pride.

"Then we went back to the tower and found the second note and the key," Benny explained. "Can you help us figure out where the treasure is buried?"

"I don't know," said Professor Meyer. "It's very mysterious, isn't it? I remember a long time ago . . ." She went off on a long story about the old days. When she'd finished, she looked at her watch. "Oh, my, look what time it is. Well, I've imposed on your hospitality long enough." She pushed her chair back from the table and stood up.

The family walked Professor Meyer to

the door. "So you don't have any more ideas about how we can find this treasure?" Benny asked, disappointed.

"No, I really don't," she said.

"Okay," Benny said, looking sad.

Professor Meyer thought for a moment. "There is one thing," she said slowly. "Let me see the second letter again."

Violet handed it to her.

The professor studied the letter. "No, I can't be sure," she said to herself. "But it could be . . ."

"What?" Benny asked excitedly.

Professor Meyer pointed to the letter. "See here where he talks about North and South?"

The children nodded.

"Morrill Hall and McGraw Hall used to be called North Building and South Building because of where they're located on the Quad," she said. "Maybe that's what he means by North and South." Professor Meyer looked around at the children. "Who knows?"

A moment later, she was gone.

"That was a lovely dinner you children made," Grandfather said. "And I certainly enjoyed having the chance to talk to Professor Meyer some more."

"I wonder if she's right about North and South meaning Morrill and McGraw," said Benny.

"In the letter, Chambers says, 'Set yourself between North and South,'" Violet said. "It sounds as if he's telling his son to stand between those two buildings."

"That's where the treasure is?" Benny asked.

"I guess so," said Henry.

"Come on, let's go!" Benny cried.

"Wait a minute, wait a minute," Henry said. "The letter says to stand there when the clock strikes six in the morning."

"But why does it matter?" Benny asked.

"I don't know," said Henry. "But that's what the letter says."

"It looks like we're getting up early tomorrow!" said Jessie.

CHAPTER 8

The Tower Points the Way

"Jessie, Violet, wake up," said Benny.

Violet opened her eyes and sat up. "What time is it?"

"Five-thirty," said Benny.

"Ugh," said Violet, falling back onto her pillow.

Benny had set his little alarm clock for five-thirty to give them time to get dressed and get to the Quad by six. He and Henry had already put on their clothes.

Jessie sprang out of bed. "Come on, Violet! Let's go find the treasure!"

The children reached the Quad a few minutes before six. They walked past the building under construction, with its wooden frame and piles of dirt. When they had reached the lawn in between McGraw and Morrill Halls, they stopped and looked around.

"I feel as if we should be looking for something," Violet said, "but I'm not sure what."

"I know what you mean," Jessie agreed.

Then they heard the clock strike. *Ding, ding, ding,* it began. The children looked around. *Ding, ding,* it continued. *Ding.* The last chime hung in the air.

"Well?" Benny asked. "The clock has struck six. Now what?"

"I don't know," said Henry.

"Let's look at the letter again," suggested Violet.

"I'm hot," said Benny. It was an unusually hot day and he had run straight up the hill to the Quad because he was so excited. "Let's sit down in the shade while we read it." He walked over and sat down in the shadow of the tower, which cut across the Quad in a long line.

As they all sat down, Violet pulled out the letter. "It says, 'The tower will point the way.' What does that mean?"

Suddenly Jessie said, "That's it! Look at the tower's shadow!"

The shadow was a long thin rectangle, with a point at the top because of the pointed roof.

"Oh, my goodness!" Violet exclaimed. "It looks like a giant arrow."

"It really is pointing the way!" Benny said.

"It looks like it's pointing to a spot right here," Henry said, marking the ground with his foot.

"That must be where it's buried!" said Jessie.

"And that would explain why we had to be here at six on a summer morning — the tower's shadow would be different at different times of the year and different times of the day," Henry pointed out.

The children looked at one another, their faces glowing with excitement.

"What are we waiting for?" Benny cried. "Let's start digging!"

"I don't think we can just start digging up the middle of the Quad," Violet said uncertainly.

"No, I don't think so, either," said Henry.

"But we can't just do nothing!" Benny said. "There's a treasure down there."

"There *might* be a treasure," Jessie reminded him. "Someone might already have found it."

"We need to ask someone if it's okay to dig," Henry said.

"Look at that truck." Violet pointed off to the side of the Quad, where some men in green jumpsuits were trimming bushes. "It says 'Goldwin University Grounds Crew' on the side. They might be good people to ask."

The children ran over to where the men were working. Jessie noticed that one of the men had a walkie-talkie and a clipboard. He seemed to be in charge. When she got closer she saw his jumpsuit had the words HEAD GROUNDSKEEPER embroidered over the left breast pocket.

"Excuse me," she said to the man. "We have a question to ask you."

"What can I do for you, young lady?" he asked.

"I know this is going to sound strange, but we'd like to dig a hole in the Quad, over there where the tower's shadow ends." Jessie turned and pointed. "Would that be okay?"

"What are you doing, searching for buried treasure?" the man asked, chuckling. "Normally I'd say no, but they're going to be digging up this area anyway this week, to put in a water line for the new construction. So it's fine with me!"

"Thank you!" Jessie said.

"You can even borrow our shovels, if you like," he said, motioning to some shovels in the back of the truck.

Jessie looked around at the others.

"That would be great," Henry said as he and Jessie each took two large shovels out of the truck. "We'll bring them back in a little while."

The four children walked back to the spot between Morrill and McGraw, carrying the shovels. When they got to the spot where the shadow seemed to be pointing, they started digging. Henry pushed his shovel in first, pulling up a big pile of dirt. The others joined in.

All of a sudden Benny stopped shoveling.

"What's the matter, Benny?" Jessie asked as she lifted a shovelful of dirt and dumped it in the growing pile.

"I was just thinking about Professor Meyer's glasses," Benny said, going back to his digging.

"Why were you thinking about that?" Henry asked.

"Remember last night I said her glasses were the same as Mrs. McGregor's?" Benny said.

The other children nodded.

"I just realized something. That's not why

they looked familiar. It's because they're the same glasses we found up in the clock tower," he said.

"Really?" Jessie asked. "That would mean Professor Meyer has been up in the tower at night. Maybe *she* dropped the letter!"

"Remember when we showed her the letter?" Violet asked. "She said, 'So that's what happened to it.' "

"And she wears sneakers," Benny said excitedly. "That would explain that muddy footprint."

"Maybe this is the 'special project' she'd said she was working on," Henry said. "Remember — she said she was always hoping to make a little more money. Finding a treasure would certainly do that!"

"But she seems so nice," Jessie said. "I can't believe she would be up to no good."

"And how could she find a treasure if she can't even find her own glasses?" Benny asked.

"Maybe that's just an act," said Henry. "Maybe she just pretends to be nice and sweet and forgetful, when she really knows exactly what she's doing."

By now they had dug a hole about a foot deep. But there was no sign of a treasure.

"What if this isn't the right spot?" Benny asked, taking a break and leaning on his shovel. It was hard work, and the children were all getting tired and sweaty.

"Or what if the treasure is already gone?" asked Violet.

"Let's dig a little while longer before we give up," Henry suggested.

"Okay," the others agreed.

A moment later, Jessie's shovel hit something hard. "I think there's something down here," she said excitedly. The others began digging in that spot as quickly as they could.

"Yes, there's definitely something hard here!" Violet said.

But when they'd pushed the dirt away, all they found was a large rock.

"Oh, no!" Benny said. "All that work for nothing. I bet it's not here."

Refusing to stop, Henry pushed his shovel into the ground one more time. The children all heard a loud clanging sound.

"What was that?" asked Benny.

"I don't know, but it didn't sound like dirt, and it didn't sound like a rock," said Henry.

Jessie, Violet, and Benny all came over and helped dig. At last they could see what Henry's shovel had hit. It was the top of a large metal box!

"The treasure!" Benny cried.

"I don't believe it," said Jessie. "It's really here!"

Getting down on their hands and knees, the children used their hands to clear the dirt away from the top and sides of the metal box. Then they dug more around the sides, until at last they had found the bottom corners of the box. After a little more digging, Henry and Jessie were able to reach down and put their arms around the big box, and put their hands underneath. "It's heavy," Henry said as he and Jessie slowly lifted.

"Yeah," Jessie gasped. Slowly the two lifted the large metal box out of the hole.

"Wow, look at that," said Violet.

The front of the box had a large heavy lock on it. "It's a good thing we have the key," said Benny.

"Let's hope it fits," Violet said, pulling it from her pocket.

She slipped the key into the old lock and turned. The lock clicked open.

The children looked at one another with anticipation. What would they find inside?

"Here goes," Henry said. He and Jessie stood on either side of the box and slowly lifted the heavy lid.

Inside the box they found several bundles wrapped in cloth. Henry bent down and began unwrapping one. Inside was an antique silver teapot. He unwrapped another bundle and found a collection of silverware. A large cloth bag was filled with heavy gold and silver coins and jewelry.

The children just stood and stared, too stunned to speak. They had known they were on a treasure hunt, but they had never imagined they'd really find a treasure.

"I don't believe it!" said Jessie.

"A real treasure," said Benny.

"But it's not ours," Violet pointed out.

"No, we'll have to return it to Joshua Chambers's family," said Henry.

"But still, I can't believe we found a real treasure," said Benny.

"You sure did," said a voice behind them. "And you beat me to it!"

The children turned to see Julia Meyer standing behind them.

"Professor Meyer!" said Henry.

CHAPTER 9

The Professor's Secret Project

The children looked at Professor Meyer and then looked at one another. Was she after the treasure?

"I thought about that second letter all night," Professor Meyer said. "When I woke up this morning, I realized that the shadow of the tower would point to the treasure! I came here as quickly as I could."

"Are you here for the treasure?" Benny asked boldly. "Is this what you meant by your 'special project'?"

"Indeed it is," the professor said with a

mysterious smile. "But not the way you think. We need to talk. Please come up to the top of the clock tower with me. Bring the box."

The children weren't sure what to do. For a moment, they just stood there. Was Professor Meyer trying to steal the treasure?

At last Henry spoke up. "Come on. Let's go see what Professor Meyer has to tell us."

First Violet ran over to return the shovels to the grounds crew. Then Henry and Jessie each picked up a side of the treasure box and carried it along with them. When they reached the bottom of the tower, they put the box down to rest their arms.

The children climbed the winding stairs very slowly, because of the treasure box. They stopped a couple of times so that Henry and Jessie could put the box down and rest.

At last they reached the top of the tower. As Professor Meyer pushed the door open, they were surprised to see their grandfather, Joel, and Don all waiting inside. Ezra was

there, too, having just finished the morning concert.

"Hello, children!" Grandfather said. "What have you got there?" The adults all crowded around the heavy metal box, which still had clumps of dirt clinging to it.

"Grandfather! Wait until you see!" Benny cried.

"What are you doing here?" Jessie asked.

"I got a phone call from Professor Meyer this morning asking me to meet her here," he explained. "Joel and Don were over having coffee, so they came along."

Grandfather looked at the box. "Is this the treasure you were hunting for?"

"It is!" cried Benny. "It really is!"

"What? You found the treasure? Where?" Don exclaimed. He was walking slowly around the large box, looking at it curiously.

"In the Quad," Jessie said. "The grounds-keeper lent us shovels and we dug it up!"

"Let's open it!" Don said.

Slowly Henry lifted the lid of the box, revealing the cloth-wrapped bundles. One by one, he unwrapped the bundles for everyone to see. Don bent over and picked each piece up, turning it over in his hands, but saying nothing.

"Look at that beautiful pocket watch!" Ezra said.

"That silver goblet is stunning," said the professor.

"But how did you know the children were going to find this treasure?" Grandfather asked.

"Remember they showed me the letters last night?" Professor Meyer began. "I didn't figure out everything that second letter meant until this morning. I looked out at the sunrise and suddenly everything fell into place! I realized that the tower's shadow would point the way! When I called, I was planning to tell them, but they'd already figured it out. They're your grandchildren, Jimmy, so I should have known they'd be smart. I asked you to join me here so that I could tell you about my project."

"Yes, please, tell us," Jessie said.

"I have been treasure hunting myself," she began.

"We thought so!" Benny cried.

Jessie explained. "We found this letter up here in the tower, and we saw lights in the middle of the night. So we figured out that someone was up here looking for the treasure. And when we found your glasses . . ."

"But I was not searching for the sort of treasure you see before you," Professor Meyer went on. "I have been searching for information about the past."

"Why are you looking for that?" Benny asked.

"I am writing a book," the professor said. "A history of Goldwin University."

"Is that how you're going to make money?" asked Jessie.

"Yes, a little bit, if I can sell a few copies," Professor Meyer said. "I have done a great deal of research. Some of my research has been up here, looking at these old photos."

"So that's when you left your glasses up here!" Henry said.

"Indeed I did," Professor Meyer said. "But I haven't been up here late at night. I've only come during the day. Much of my research has been speaking with people connected with Goldwin. One such person is Laurence Chambers, the great-great-grandnephew of the university's first president, Joshua Chambers." The professor paused and looked around. "He told me an interesting tale. He said that all of the family's valuables were mysteriously missing after the Civil War. There was a story in the family that his great-great-granduncle, Joshua Chambers, had hidden them to keep them safe from the army. But no one ever knew for sure what had happened to them. So when I read that letter last night, it answered a lot of questions — but raised many more."

"Is that why you said, 'So that's what happened to it,' when we showed you the letters?" Violet said.

"Yes," the professor said. "I had been wondering where the family wealth had gone."

"But if you weren't the one who had the letter in the first place," Henry said, "then who did?"

"And who was up here in the middle of the night?" asked Jessie.

Just then the door burst open and Andi came rushing in. She seemed surprised by the crowd of people in the tower. She looked even more surprised when she saw the silver and gold objects laid out on the desk.

"Look at the treasure we found!" Benny said.

"You found this?" Andi asked. "Where? How?"

"We found two letters with clues in them — " Benny began, but before he could explain, Andi burst out crying. She dropped her bag and sank down in a chair, her face in her hands.

"Miss Barton!" Ezra said. "What is the matter?"

Andi took a deep breath and tried to collect herself. She looked around at all the faces staring at her.

"I'm sorry, it's nothing . . ." she began.

Jessie whispered to Henry, "Do you think she's upset because she was the one looking for the treasure?"

Henry shrugged his shoulders.

"Oh, Ezra," Andi was saying. "I'm upset because I came here to quit. I can't be your assistant anymore."

"But whyever not?" Ezra asked.

"Because I'm no good," Andi said. "I keep losing things, like the new music I bought. And I don't play well enough. I've been sneaking in here for extra practice, but I didn't want you to know."

"Don't play well enough?" Ezra said. "You're great! In fact, you're so good, I'm afraid they're going to give you my job when you graduate! I'm getting old, and you're bringing in that exciting newfangled music."

"I thought you didn't like the new music," Andi said.

Ezra looked at her sheepishly. "I admit it took me a little while to get used to the idea. But now I really enjoy it." He paused. "In fact, the reason you couldn't find your music is because I borrowed it." He looked at the Aldens. "I may be the one you've seen up here at night. I came up here once to try out Miss Barton's new music, but I didn't want anyone to know."

Andi beamed. "I'm so relieved. I thought you were disappointed with me."

"Well, you could try to be a little more organized," Ezra said. "But you're an excellent carillon player."

"I'll try harder," Andi said. "And I'll help you with the new music. I'm just so honored to be working with a gifted carillon player like you."

"Now we know who was up in the tower those nights," Henry said.

"Actually, I only came up here one night," Ezra said.

The children looked at one another, confused. "But we saw a light up here on two different nights."

At that moment Don came forward and cleared his throat. "I think I have some explaining to do," he said. "I was the one you saw up here in the tower the other night."

CHAPTER 10

A Reward for the Children

"*You* were the one?" Joel asked in disbelief.

"Yes, I was the one who found the letter — and then left it up here," Don said.

"Where did you find it?" Benny wanted to know.

"It was tucked inside that antique book my father gave me," Don said.

"So that's why you didn't want us looking at the book," Jessie said.

"That's right — I kept the letter in the book," he said. "Until I brought it up here.

I didn't want you looking in the book because I was afraid you might see it."

"That day we saw you on the Quad and you started to ask us about the book — " Jessie recalled.

"By then I'd realized I'd lost the letter," Don said. "I was going to ask if you had seen it. But then I decided I'd better not mention it, or I'd have a lot of explaining to do."

Then Joel spoke up. "So that's why you were so eager to come up here to visit. You wanted to find the treasure."

"Yes," Don said. "I went up into the tower in the middle of the night to search. I only had a flashlight on, so I didn't think anyone would see me."

Suddenly Violet remembered something. "It was your muddy footprint we saw, wasn't it?" she said, looking down at the sneakers Don was wearing.

"I suppose it must have been," Don agreed. "When I was searching around up here, I tried to look inside and behind the carillon — I'm afraid I may have broken some of the wires by accident when I leaned on them. I even went up to look at the bells and unscrewed some of the parts to see if somehow a treasure could be hidden inside."

"That was a terrible thing you did," Ezra said angrily. "It took me a long time to fix the carillon."

Don's face turned red, and he looked at the floor. "I'm so sorry," he said quietly. "I wasn't thinking. I'd come so far, and I didn't want to leave empty-handed. I'll repay you for the time you spent repairing them."

"What I don't understand is: Why were you being so secretive? Why not tell the university what you'd found?" Professor Meyer asked.

"I know what I did wasn't right. But I never intended to keep the money. I just wanted to find the treasure." Don looked at his father.

"Still playing detective?" Joel asked.

"I guess so," Don said sadly. "I'm sorry."

"Well, I'm glad all the mysteries have

been solved," the professor said. "Thanks to the Aldens." She smiled at the children, who smiled back proudly.

"What's going to happen to the treasure?" Benny asked.

"We'll have to notify the Chambers family," Professor Meyer said. "For now, perhaps, we should bring the treasure to the president's office for safekeeping."

"That sounds like a good idea," said Jessie.

The next day, the Aldens were getting ready to leave Goldwin and return home. Their suitcases were packed and ready. The family was just finishing up lunch in the dining hall.

"I've enjoyed being here again after all these years, but it will be good to get back to Greenfield," Grandfather said.

"I agree," said Jessie.

"I miss Mrs. McGregor's cooking," Benny said.

"Look, there's Professor Meyer," Violet called out as they stood up to leave.

Grandfather waved to her and she came right over. "I'm glad I found you before you left," she said. "I spoke with Laurence Chambers last night. He was overjoyed to hear that you had found the family valuables — he couldn't believe it. In fact, he took the first flight here and arrived this morning."

"Really?" Henry said. "Has he seen the treasure yet?"

"Yes, and it was more wonderful than he'd imagined," the professor said. "He'd like to meet you and thank you in person."

The children looked at one another, their eyes glowing.

"We'd love to," said Jessie.

The Aldens went with the professor up to the top of the tower one last time. When they reached the top, a tall dark-haired man was standing looking out the window. As he turned to face them, Violet said, "You look like your great-great-granduncle."

"Do I?" Mr. Chambers asked.

"Yes," Henry agreed. "We saw a picture of him in a book."

"And you must be the Aldens," Mr. Chambers said. "I can't thank you enough for finding my family heirlooms."

"It was our pleasure," Jessie assured him.

"I'd like to give each of you a small piece of the treasure," Mr. Chambers went on. He held out his hand and showed the children four old gold coins. "Will you accept these as your reward?"

The children were too stunned to speak. As he handed each of them a coin, Grandfather said, "They're speechless. I think that means they accept your offer."

At last the children remembered their manners. "Thank you!" they each said.

"As I was saying, it is the sentimental value, not the money, that matters to me," Mr. Chambers said. "Last night I discussed with my family what to do with this treasure.

"As you know, my family has always been very devoted to this university. We will keep a few pieces, but the rest we are going to donate to Goldwin. We'll be putting some of the antiques, like the goblets, on display."

"What about the gold and silver?" asked Henry.

"My cousins and I discussed what to do with it," Mr. Chambers said. "My great-great-granduncle was quite fond of music, especially the carillon. You may have figured that out from his letters."

"Yes, it sounded that way," said Jessie.

"My family would like to use this money to add some new bells," said Mr. Chambers.

"What a wonderful idea," Ezra said. "Thank you so very much."

"Our music will sound even more beautiful," Andi said excitedly.

"Your great-great-granduncle would have been proud," Ezra said.

"Thank you for calling me," Mr. Chambers said to Professor Meyer. Then he turned to the Aldens. "And thank you again, for finding my family's treasure."

"You're welcome," said Henry.

"Anytime you need a treasure found, just call us!" said Benny with a smile. "We're always ready for a treasure hunt."

GERTRUDE CHANDLER WARNER discovered when she was teaching that many readers who like an exciting story could find no books that were both easy and fun to read. She decided to try to meet this need, and her first book, *The Boxcar Children*, quickly proved she had succeeded.

Miss Warner drew on her own experiences to write the mystery. As a child she spent hours watching trains go by on the tracks opposite her family home. She often dreamed about what it would be like to set up housekeeping in a caboose or freight car — the situation the Alden children find themselves in.

When Miss Warner received requests for more adventures involving Henry, Jessie, Violet, and Benny Alden, she began additional stories. In each, she chose a special setting and introduced unusual or eccentric characters who liked the unpredictable.

While the mystery element is central to each of Miss Warner's books, she never thought of them as strictly juvenile mysteries. She liked to stress the Aldens' independence and resourcefulness and their solid New England devotion to using up and making do. The Aldens go about most of their adventures with as little adult supervision as possible — something else that delights young readers.

Miss Warner lived in Putnam, Connecticut, until her death in 1979. During her lifetime, she received hundreds of letters from girls and boys telling her how much they liked her books.